ANASTASIA MOORE

Copyright © 2021 by Anastasia Moore

BY

All rights reserved.

No part of this publication may be reproduced or transmitted

in any form or by any means electronic or mechanical,

including photocopy, recording, or any information storage

and retrieval system now known or invented, without permission

in writing from the publisher, except by a reviewer who wishes

to quote brief passages in connection with a review written

for inclusion in a magazine, newspaper, or broadcast.

Print ISBN: 978-1-66780-394-4

Printed in the United States of America

Dedication from Anastasia ("Boy") Moore, Author

This story is dedicated to my late father.
May the love and support you invested in your little girl spread
to all who read this story and inspire them to discover their wings.
"If you're a Moore, you'll make it!" – George W. Moore

Dedication from Wendy Thompson, Illustrator

In loving memory of my daughter, Lindsay, and also my Dad.
Special thanks to Mr. Louie, whose influence made this happen.

Hi, my name is Boy,
and I'm eight whole years old.
Even though I'm just one little girl,
I'm sure to break the mold.
There are so many things I want to be.
I can't wait to grow up; I want to see.
With my daddy here beside me,
there's no telling who I'll be.
The whole wide world is open and free.

This is my daddy.
He's super old and knows lots of cool stuff.
He always tells me that we're friends
'til the end and that our time together
will never be enough. Most people call him
"Bird," so I guess he has to have wings somewhere,

but to me, he's just my daddy,
who makes me comb my hair.

No, I'm not an average girl,
and that's how I got my name.
Things would be so boring
if we all were just the same.
I like biking, fishing, dressing up,
and playing house.
I believe I could enjoy any game.
Daddy tells me that we're all different,
and I can I like all these things,
without a drop of shame.
Sometimes I sit and imagine
who I will be someday.
My daddy always tells me
that I'll be someone great,
no matter what, come what may.

When daddy gets home
from a long day at work,
he makes time just for me.

He kicks off his big boots,
we climb in his favorite chair,
and he sneaks me chocolate,
so mama won't see.

I laugh at all his stories about
when he was little, just like me.
He tells me about all his adventures
and about how he and mama came to be.
Daddy says: "Enough about me, Boy.
Although I'm glad you got my sense of humor.
Now, tell me more about all the things
that you want to do in the future."

I say, "I want to be a vet,
and help animals far and wide."

Daddy says, "Let me get my hat
and my keys and I'll show you
where they hide.
Some animals live in houses
and some live far away.
I'll bring you your first few patients
that I've found along the way."

I say, "I want to be a lawyer,
and give those bad guys the boot."

Daddy says, "My Boy, if you're willing
to stand up for the innocent,
I'll gladly buy you a suit.

You'll need to study hard and look professional
when you approach the judge.

So, prepare in advance to build a case
that simply won't budge.

We'll practice asking questions.
I'll pretend to be your witness.

You'll get better each and every day
and then justice will be your business."

I say, "I want to be a construction worker
and build people the homes
of their wildest dreams."

Daddy says, "First I'll teach you the names
of the tools, then we can be a team.

We'll start here at home with nails,
hammers, screwdrivers, and screws.

Then one day when you've mastered that,
you'll have your own construction crews.

I say, "I want to be an explorer
who goes on adventures and climbs
with all my might."
Daddy says, "I'll memorize the map for you
to be sure you get there alright.
I'll memorize the highways
and all the routes that you'll take.
I'll be just one phone call away to help
with any mistake you make.
I'll check on you every now and then
to be sure you'll still having fun.
I want you to laugh, sing, and dance,
yet don't forget to play and run."

I say, "I want to be a therapist
and help people find their smile."

Daddy says, "I'll be your first patient
because your daddy hasn't smiled in a while.

You know your daddy loves you
but sometimes I get really sad.

It's nice to have someone like you
to talk to, it brings me back to being
your number-one dad."

I say, "I want to be a doctor
and help sick people get healthy.
I want to help people to feel better,
not to become wealthy."

Daddy says, "Sometimes people
get sick so quick.
You can't save them all.
It's the love you have and thought
that counts that make
your daddy proud and want to stand tall."

I say, "I want to be an author
and write stories with lots of lessons to glean.
I want to write the stories to help
other kids think big and build their self-esteem."
Daddy says, "I never learned to read or write,
so, what I do is dream. Now, write your stories
and fill hundreds of books. Write them
for you and me. Write for all who couldn't
and who never got to sparkle or gleam.

Although I'm not here with you,
I love you just the same.

These are the wings that once belonged to me,
the ones that earned me my name.

Bird is what they called me,
but I never got to fly.

So, now I give them to you, my dear, Boy,
because when it came to dreaming,
we always saw eye to eye.

I won't be here to see it,
but I know you'll make me proud.
Take these wings, continue to dream,
and now I know you'll see,
I want you to be the best,
my Boy, that you can ever be!"